*The*

*Bears
On
Hemlock
Mountain*

# The
# *Bears*
# *On*
# *Hemlock*
# *Mountain*

by ALICE DALGLIESH

lllustrated by HELEN SEWELL

ALADDIN PAPERBACKS
New York  London  Toronto  Sydney  Singapore

The outline of this story was kindly given to me by
Colonel Henry Shoemaker, State Archivist of Pennsylvania,
who collects "tales told by the people."

He has granted me permission to use it, and I have given it
more detail and form. The central element, however—the story
of the boy, the bear and the iron pot, is unchanged. It is, of
course, a small "tall tale."

Third Aladdin Paperbacks edition May 2000
Second Aladdin Paperbacks edition 1992
First Aladdin Paperbacks edition 1981

Aladdin Paperbacks
An imprint of Simon & Schuster Children's Publishing
1230 Avenue of the Americas
New York, NY 10020

Library of Congress Cataloging-in-Publication Data
Dalgliesh, Alice.
The bears on Hemlock mountain / by Alice Dalgliesh; illustrated
By Helen Sewell—3rd Aladdin Paperbacks ed.
p.   cm.
Summary: A young boy sent on an errand over Hemlock Mountain is not so sure he
likes going alone, because there may be bears on the mountain, but with the help of
the big iron pot he borrows, he completes his errand.
ISBN-13: 978-0-689-71604-1 (ISBN-10: 0-689-71604-4)
[1. Bears—Fiction.] I. Sewell, Helen, date. ill. II. Title.
PZ7.D153Be  1992
[E]—dc20  91-40166

TO JONATHAN NOON

# CHAPTER 1

## About Jonathan

Jonathan lived in a gray stone farmhouse at the foot of Hemlock Mountain. Now Hemlock Mountain was not a mountain at all, it was a hill, and not a very big one. But someone had started calling it Hemlock Mountain, and the name had stuck. Now everyone talked about "going over Hemlock Mountain."

It was the year when Jonathan was eight that he went over Hemlock Mountain. He was a fine big boy for his age. That was why his mother could send him over the Mountain all by himself.

The winter had been a cold one. Even now, in early spring, there was snow on the ground. The birds and the squirrels and the rabbits had a hard time finding anything to eat, so every day Jonathan remembered to feed them. Jonathan loved animals and birds. He knew the tracks that each one made in the snow.

The small creatures could not find enough to eat, but it was not so with Jonathan's aunts and uncles and cousins. All they had to do was to come to the gray stone farmhouse and there was always plenty of food. Jonathan's mother was a fine cook and all

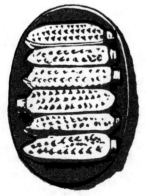

the aunts, uncles and cousins knew it. They liked to drop in for supper and to sit around the table in front of the big fireplace.

Such good suppers! There would be roast chicken or roast duck or roast goose, brown and done to a turn. There would be potatoes and turnips, carrots and corn. And of course there would be pies—pumpkin and apple and squash. While for those who like cookies, there were crisp brown ones cut into every shape you can imagine.

Jonathan's mother liked company but sometimes—oh, once in a while—she wished they did not have so much of it. Or that the aunts and uncles and cousins were not quite so hungry.

## CHAPTER 2

## Young Uncle James

Jonathan was very fond of his uncles. He was fond of his cousins and his aunts. It was pretty fine for a boy to have so many uncles and aunts. If all his uncles and aunts stood side by side they would go all the way from the house to the gate—or very nearly.

He liked all the uncles, but best of all he liked young Uncle James. Young Uncle James was only fourteen years old, so he and Jonathan were friends.

Young Uncle James had eyes that saw and ears that heard.

"Look," he would say to Jonathan. "Down by that tree stump is a cottontail."

Then he and Jonathan were very still.

They could see the little brown rabbit washing his face and his ears.

"Listen," young Uncle James would say. "There is a song sparrow. Do you hear what he says?"

Then he and Jonathan were very still. They could see the song sparrow singing on a branch. And the song sparrow was saying, over and over again,

"Put on the kettle, kettle, kettle!"

Once Jonathan and Uncle James went down to the brook. It was late in the day and the shadows were long.

"What are we going to see?" asked Jonathan.

"Wait and you will find out," said Uncle James.

So they waited and listened. It was hard for Jonathan to keep so still.

They waited and listened. And at last a raccoon came down to the brook. He had an apple in his mouth.

"Look!" said Uncle James. "Look carefully, Jonathan."

Jonathan looked. The raccoon took the apple in his two front paws. He dipped it in the water and dipped it and dipped it and dipped it again.

"'Coons like their food wet," said Uncle James.

That was the way of it. Every day Jonathan and Uncle James listened and looked. They never threw sticks at the animals, or scared the birds. Soon all the animals and

birds were their friends. The squirrel was the best friend of all. He came very near to get nuts from Jonathan.

"Uncle James," said Jonathan. "Did you ever see a bear?"

"Well, now," said Uncle James, looking important. "I believe I did. But it was years ago, Jonathan."

"How many years ago?"

"Before you were born. Yes, it was before you were born."

"I would like to see a bear," said Jonathan. "I would rather see a bear than anything in the world."

"Maybe you will!" said Uncle James.

That was all he said. But Jonathan kept on thinking about bears.

CHAPTER 3

The Iron Pot

Now if there are lots of aunts and uncles there are likely to be lots of new cousins. Jonathan kept having new cousins all the time.

It happened that a new small cousin of Jonathan's was being christened. So, of course, all the aunts and uncles and older cousins were going to the christening. Afterwards, so they thought, it would be fine to have supper in the gray stone farmhouse.

It was fine when relatives came in ones and twos, or threes and fours, or even in fives and sixes. But this particular time twenty of them were coming.

"Twenty of them!" said Jonathan's mother.

"Whatever shall we do?"

"Give them a good, big, hearty stew," said Jonathan's father. "Fill 'em up with it and then give 'em cookies. That should be enough."

"It's a fine idea," said Jonathan's mother as she rolled out the cookie dough and cut it into stars and bells, hearts and flowers, rabbits and birds and a dozen other things.

"A fine idea. But where in all the world shall I get a pot big enough to make a stew for twenty—no, twenty-three—people? For of course you and Jonathan and I must be counted in."

"I should think so!" Jonathan's father said. "And remember I am very hungry this cold weather."

He certainly was.

But then he was a big man and worked hard on the farm. Even in the wintertime he worked hard, for there were the cows to be milked and all the other animals to be fed. There was wood to be cut. This kept the big fire going so that Jonathan's mother could cook all the good things the family liked to eat. Jonathan helped carry in the wood.

Jonathan's mother kept thinking about the stew and about the pot that would be big enough to cook it.

"I know!" she said to Jonathan, as he brought in an armful of wood, "your aunt Emma, over across Hemlock Mountain, has the biggest iron pot you ever laid eyes on."

"*I* never laid eyes on it," said Jonathan.

"Then you are going to," said his mother.

"Your father is much too busy to go for it, but you can go and fetch it."

"Me?" said Jonathan. "All alone? They say there are bears on Hemlock Mountain."

"Stuff and nonsense," said his mother. "Many's the time I've been over Hemlock Mountain and not a bear did I see. Your Uncle James must have been telling you stories. Besides if there *were* bears they'd be asleep this time of year. And besides there *are* no bears."

"But it's a long way and the pot is heavy," Jonathan said. "And bears wake up in the spring."

"You are a big boy, now," his mother told him. "Get on your warm coat and your warm cap and your warm muffler and go

quickly, for you must be back before it is dark. Tomorrow, early, I shall start the stew."

So Jonathan put on his coat and his muffler and pulled his warm cap down over his ears. He filled his pockets full of nuts for the squirrels on Hemlock Mountain, and he took some bread crumbs for the birds.

Then Jonathan went tramping to the gate, his boots making big footprints in the snow. Crunch! Crunch! Crunch! Then suddenly he turned and went back.

"Ma," he said when his mother opened
the door, "will you give me some carrots?"

"Some carrots? Whatever for?"

"For the rabbits on Hemlock Mountain.
I have nuts for the squirrels, and bread
crumbs for the birds. Now I want carrots
for the rabbits."

"Well, of course," said his mother, and she gave him a bunch of carrots. Then she went to the cookie jar and brought out a handful of cookies.

"And these are for you," she said. "Just in case you should be late coming over the mountain. But you must not be late, for it still gets dark early."

"Thank you," said Jonathan, and he put the cookies in his pocket. "I won't be late, because
        MAYBE
            THERE ARE BEARS
                ON HEMLOCK MOUNTAIN!"

Then he was off again, crunch, crunch, crunch in his big boots, making big footprints all the way to the gate.

## CHAPTER 4

## Up Hemlock Mountain

When Jonathan was out of sight of the house, his mother began to worry just a little bit about bears on Hemlock Mountain.

Stuff and nonsense, she said to herself. There *are* no bears on Hemlock Mountain. But perhaps . . . She went back to her cookie making and tried to forget about it.

But she couldn't forget. She found she was cutting out cookies to a kind of rhythm:

There *are* no bears on

Hemlock    Mountain

No bears at all

Of course there are no

bears on Hemlock Mountain

No bears, no bears, no bears, no bears at all.

Jonathan went up Hemlock Mountain eating a cookie as he went.

It was very still on Hemlock Mountain. The only sound was Jonathan's boots going crunch, crunch, crunch on the snow. He could look back and see the big footprints that he made. It was very lonely. So lonely that Jonathan made up words to go with the crunch, crunch of his boots. Strangely enough they were the same words as his mother's:

THERE *are* NO BEARS

ON HEMLOCK MOUNTAIN,

NO BEARS AT ALL.

OF COURSE THERE ARE NO BEARS
ON HEMLOCK MOUNTAIN,
NO BEARS, NO BEARS, NO BEARS,
NO BEARS AT ALL.

When he got to the top of Hemlock Mountain, Jonathan was out of breath. So he sat down on a log to rest. And as he rested he took out of his pocket the nuts and the carrots and the bread crumbs. He put them on the snow a little distance from where he was sitting.

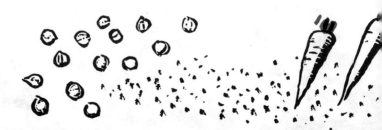

It was very still and quiet. To keep up his courage Jonathan said to himself:

THERE *are*

NO BEARS

ON HEMLOCK MOUNTAIN,

NO BEARS AT ALL.

THERE ARE NO BEARS

ON HEMLOCK MOUNTAIN,

NO BEARS, NO BEARS, NO BEARS,

NO BEARS

AT ALL.

Then there began to be little sounds all around him. And out of the woods came rabbits, hopping over the snow. They came straight to the carrots Jonathan had brought for them.

Out of the woods came squirrels. They looked around with bright eyes, and put one paw on their hearts, the way squirrels do. Then they came straight to the nuts Jonathan had brought for them.

And then came the winter birds, hopping and twittering. They came straight to the bread crumbs Jonathan had brought for them.

Jonathan sat as still as still. He was not lonely now. And he was not worried about bears. He had lots of company. For quite

a long time he sat there watching the rabbits and the squirrels and the birds.

But time was going on and the sun was
lower in the sky.

Jonathan knew he must be on his way.
So he got to his feet, and his boots went
crunch, crunch, crunch on the snow.

All the rabbits went hopping back to the
woods. The squirrels looked around with
their paws on their hearts. Then, whisk! and
away up the trees. The birds flew up into
the branches. Jonathan was alone.

## CHAPTER 5

## Down Hemlock Mountain

Now Jonathan started down the other side of Hemlock Mountain. It was very still and his boots went crunch, crunch, crunch on the snow. Jonathan could look back and see the endless footprints he was making.

It was quiet, so quiet! To keep up his courage Jonathan said to himself, marking time to the sound of his steps on the snow:

THERE *are* NO BEARS
    ON HEMLOCK MOUNTAIN,

NO BEARS, NO BEARS AT ALL,

OF COURSE THERE ARE NO BEARS
    ON HEMLOCK MOUNTAIN.

NO BEARS, NO BEARS, NO BEARS, NO BEARS
    AT ALL.

He went down the mountain much faster than he had come up. At the bottom he stopped and looked back at the enormous footprints he had made in the snow. There were no other footprints, not any at all. Jonathan had been the only one on Hemlock Mountain. It made him feel lonesome just to think of it.

And as Jonathan stood still, there was a strange, small sound. Drip, drip, drip! The sun was warm on the south side of the mountain and the snow and ice were beginning to melt. Drip, drip, drip from the branches of trees. Drip, drip, drip from the rocks.

*It sounds like spring,* Jonathan said to himself. *It feels like spring.* I HOPE THE BEARS DON'T KNOW IT!

## CHAPTER 6

### Aunt Emma's House

When Jonathan began to think about spring and about bears, it made him feel the need to hurry.

So he went on, very quickly. Down here on the other side of Hemlock Mountain the sun was even warmer. Drip, drip, drip, went the trees. Jonathan's boots no longer went crunch on the snow. They sank into it, and he made bigger footprints than before.

Soon he was at his Aunt Emma's house. By the gate some hungry birds were hopping about on the snow. Jonathan felt in his

pockets. Yes, there were a few crumbs. So he threw them to the birds and went round to the back door.

Jonathan lifted the brass knocker and let it fall. How loud it sounded! But it was a cozy, comfortable sound, not a lonely one. Jonathan had come over Hemlock Mountain and here he was, safe at his aunt's house! He began to feel big and noble and brave. Jonathan seemed to grow an inch taller as he stood waiting for his aunt to open the door.

Footsteps came hurrying through the kitchen. The door opened and there was his Aunt Emma. She was wearing a big white apron, and Jonathan hoped she had been cooking. By now he was very, very hungry.

"Mercy sakes, Jonathan!" said his Aunt Emma. "What are you doing here this snowy day? Come in!"

Jonathan went in, but first he shook the snow carefully off his boots. Aunt Emma was a good housekeeper. Then he went into the kitchen. A big fire was burning, and the kitchen was pleasant and warm. The air was full of a good smell. Jonathan sniffed — M-m-m- cookies!

It was quite hard to be polite. But Jonathan sat down in the rocker and tried not to look hungry. He had quite forgotten about the cookies eaten on the way.

"Well," said his Aunt Emma, "what brings you here?"

"I came to see you, Aunt," said Jonathan, full of politeness and hunger. The big black cat came and rubbed against his legs. Jonathan stroked her.

"Tush!" said his aunt. "You can't tell me that you came all the way over Hemlock Mountain just for a visit?" Then she looked at him sharply.

"Jonathan! *Did you come all alone over Hemlock Mountain?*"

"Yes," said Jonathan. "Why?"

"Because—" said his aunt.

"Because what?" asked Jonathan.

"Because, nothing." But Jonathan knew she was thinking about BEARS.

The cat arched her back and purred. Jonathan thought he had been polite long enough. So he allowed himself to give just a small sniff.

Sniff, sniff. "Smells good in here!" said Jonathan.

Sniff!

"Mercy's sake," said his aunt. "You must be hungry coming all the way over the Mountain. Would you like a cookie?"

"Please. Thank you," said Jonathan hoping he did not sound too eager. Hoping, too, that it would not be just *one* cookie.

He need not have worried. His aunt brought a plate with a whole pile of crisp crunchy cookies. She put them on the table beside him. Then she brought a mug and a big blue pitcher of milk.

Mm-m-m! The cookies were good! Not as good as his mother's perhaps, but *good*, just the same.

Jonathan rocked and munched on cookies. He drank milk. He rocked and munched and drank. The clock on the kitchen shelf did its best to tell him that time was passing.

"Tick-tock, tick-tock, time to go, tick-tock."

But Jonathan rocked and ate and did not hear it.

"Tick-tock, tick-tock."

The fire was warm and Jonathan was most awfully full. He stopped rocking and slowly, slowly, slowly, his eyes closed. Jonathan was asleep!

*Mercy's sakes!* thought his aunt. *I wonder what the boy wanted? But it would be a shame to wake him* . . . So she let him sleep.

## CHAPTER 7

## There May Be Bears

Time went on. Jonathan slept. The sun went lower in the sky.

"Tick-tock!" said the clock. "Time to go!" But Jonathan went on sleeping.

The big black cat had also been sleeping by the fire. Now she got up, stretched, and came to rub against Jonathan's legs.

As she rubbed she purred, a loud rumble of a purr. And then, at last, Jonathan awoke!

At first he did not know where he was. Then he remembered.

"Oh!" he said. "It is late and Ma said I must be home before dark."

"There is still time, if you hurry," said his aunt. She wondered if Jonathan had come there just to eat her cookies. Why should he when his mother made such good cookies of her own. It was quite a puzzle.

Jonathan put on his muffler and his coat and his boots.

"Goodbye Aunt Emma," he said politely.

"Goodbye Jonathan. Do not waste time going over the mountain."

"Why not?"

"Because..."

"Because what?"

"Oh, just because..."

Jonathan was quite sure she was thinking about bears. But he was brave, and off he went toward Hemlock Mountain.

Jonathan had gone quite a way before it suddenly came to him. He stood still in the snow, feeling very cross with himself. You and I know what he had forgotten.

### THE BIG IRON POT!

There was nothing for poor Jonathan to do but to turn and go back.

How silly I am, he said to himself. How silly I am!

In a short time he was back at his Aunt Emma's house. Once more he lifted the brass knocker. Aunt Emma came to the door.

"Jonathan! Did you forget something?"

"I forgot what I came for," Jonathan said truthfully. "Mom sent me to ask for the loan

of your big iron pot. After the christening all the aunts and uncles and cousins are coming to supper."

"And as I am one of them, I'll be glad to lend you my big iron pot," said Aunt Emma. She went into the kitchen and came back with the big iron pot. It was very large. Now

Jonathan did not feel as if he had grown at least an inch. He felt like a very small boy.

"Do you think you can carry it?"

"Indeed I can," said Jonathan, trying to feel big and brave again. He took the pot by the handle and started off toward Hemlock Mountain.

When he was out of sight his aunt began to worry.

"He is not very big," she told the black cat. "And it is growing dark."

"Purr-rr-rr," said the black cat. "Purr-rr-rr."

"Oh, don't tell *me*," said Jonathan's aunt with crossness in her voice.

"YOU KNOW
    THERE MAY BE BEARS
        ON HEMLOCK MOUNTAIN!"

## CHAPTER 8

## Watch Out, Jonathan!

Jonathan and the big iron pot were going up the side of Hemlock Mountain.

Now it was really beginning to be dark. Jonathan knew he should hurry, but the iron pot was heavy. Jonathan's steps were heavy and slow. This time he was stepping in the big foot-prints he had made coming down.

It was really and truly dark. The tall trees were dark. The woods were dark and scary.

"Crack!" a branch broke in the woods. It was as loud as a pistol shot.

"Woo-ooh. Woo-ooh!" That was an owl, but it was a most lonely sound.

Jonathan began to think about bears. And to keep up his courage he said, in time to his own slow steps:

THERE...ARE...NO...BEARS
        ON...HEMLOCK...MOUNTAIN
NO BEARS...NO...BEARS...AT...ALL.

He was tired and out of breath. So he rested for a minute, then he went on saying:

THERE...ARE...NO...BEARS...
        ON...HEMLOCK...MOUNTAIN.
NO BEARS...

Watch out, Jonathan. WATCH OUT! What was that, among the trees, right on top of the mountain? Two big, dark...what could they be?

They moved slowly...slowly...but they were coming nearer...and nearer ... and nearer ...

Jonathan had to think quickly. There was only one thing to be done. Jonathan did it. He put the big iron pot upside down on the snow. Then he dug out a place and crawled under it.

The pot was like a safe house. Jonathan
dug out another little place in the snow so
that he could breathe.

Then he waited.

## CHAPTER 9

### Paws on the Snow

Crunch! Crunch! Crunch! It was the sound of big, heavy paws on the snow.

The bears were coming!

Crunch! Crunch! Crunch! Nearer and nearer and nearer . . .

Jonathan's hair stood up straight on his head. He thought about a lot of things. He thought of his mother and father and the gray stone farmhouse. Had they missed him?

Would they come to look for him? He thought about the bears and wondered how they knew it was spring.

Crunch! Crunch! Crunch! Nearer and nearer . . . Jonathan made foolish words to the sound just to keep up his courage:

THERE...ARE...NO...BEARS
　　　ON...HEMLOCK...MOUNTAIN...
NO...BEARS...AT...ALL...

But the sound had stopped. The bears were *right beside the big iron pot.*

Jonathan could hear them breathing.

And he was all alone on Hemlock Mountain.

Suddenly, above the breathing of the bears, Jonathan heard a noise.

It was a twittering and a chattering. The twittering was the soft, comfortable noise that birds make before they go to sleep.

And then Jonathan knew that the trees were full of birds and squirrels. He was not alone on Hemlock Mountain.

Perhaps the bears knew this, too. Perhaps they had not quite waked up from their long winter nap. They sat there by the big iron pot. They waited and waited. But they did not try to dig under it.

Inside the iron pot it was dark. Jonathan was far from comfortable. Outside he could hear the bears going sniff, sniff, sniff. Poor Jonathan!

*Oh,* he said to himself. *Why did I wait so long at Aunt Emma's? Why did I eat so many cookies? Why did I go to sleep?* There did not seem to be any answer to these questions, so he stopped asking them.

The birds kept up their twittering and the squirrels kept up their chattering.

Sniff, sniff went the bears. One began scraping at the snow around the iron pot.

Poor Jonathan!

Then the birds stopped twittering and the squirrels stopped chattering. The bears stopped sniffing and listened. What was that?

Crunch! Crunch! Crunch!

Away off in the distance there was the sound of boots on the snow. Someone was coming up Hemlock Mountain!

It was very still. The only sound was the crunch of boots. And at last Jonathan heard it. His father's voice!

"Hello-o-o-oh, Jon-a-than!"

"Hello-o-o-oh, Pa!"

Jonathan's voice did not sound very loud under the iron pot. Would his father hear it?

Again his father's voice came, nearer and louder.

"HELLO-O-O-OH, JON-A-THAN!"

"HELLO-O-O-OH, Pa!"

The bears had had enough of this. They went lumbering off into the woods. And the crunch of boots on the snow came nearer and nearer . . .

# CHAPTER 10

## There ARE Bears

Jonathan pushed back the big iron pot and stood up.

There were no bears. But up the path came his father, carrying his gun. And with him were Jonathan's Uncle James and his Uncle Samuel, his Uncle John and his Uncle Peter. Jonathan had never in all his life been so glad to see the uncles.

"Jonathan!" said his father, "what a fright you have given us! Where have you been all this time?"

"Coming over Hemlock Mountain," said Jonathan in a small voice. And he ran right into his father's arms.

"Well," said his father, when he had finished hugging Jonathan. "What is this?" He was looking at the big iron pot. "And why is it upside down?"

"Bears," said Jonathan.

"THERE

    *are*

        BEARS ON HEMLOCK MOUNTAIN."

"Stuff and nonsense!" said his father.

"But you are carrying your gun," said Jonathan. "So is uncle . . ."

"Well. . ." said his father.

Jonathan pointed to the bear tracks in the snow.

"Bears," he said firmly.

"THERE *are*

    BEARS ON HEMLOCK MOUNTAIN."

Jonathan's father looked at the bear tracks in the snow. His uncles looked at them, too.

"So!" they said. "So-o-o!"

And the uncles went off into the woods with their guns.

"You and I must go home, Jonathan," said his father. "Your mother is worrying herself sick. You have been a mighty long time coming over Hemlock Mountain."

"Yes, Pop," said Jonathan, and he hung his head.

"But what kept you so long?" asked his father. They were going down the mountain, now, and Jonathan's father was carrying the big iron pot.

"Well," said Jonathan. "First I ate cookies, then I drank milk, then I slept . . . "

"H'm," said his father. "It is not the way to do when you are sent on an errand. But I guess you have learned that by this time."

It was very still on Hemlock Mountain.

There was only the crunch, crunch of boots on the snow. A squirrel scampered to a tree. He sat looking at Jonathan and his father, his paws on his heart.

"I know what I know!" he seemed to say.

Crack! What was that? A shot in the woods? Or a branch snapping? The squirrel, frightened, scampered higher up in the tree.

"Oh!" said Jonathan.

"Something tells me," his father said. "Something tells me we shall have bear steak for dinner!"

They kept on down the mountain. The birds twittered in the trees.

"We know what we know."

"The birds and the squirrels and the rabbits helped me," Jonathan said. "They are my friends."

"How could they help you?" asked his father. "They are so little."

"Well..." said Jonathan. But now they were near the gray stone farmhouse and there was no time to explain.

The firelight shone through the open door. It made a warm, golden path on the snow. And in the doorway was Jonathan's mother.

"Oh, Jonny!" she said, as she hugged him. "How glad I am that you are safely home!"

As for Jonathan, all he said in a rather out-of-breath way was:

"THERE . . . *are* . . . BEARS
                ON . . . HEMLOCK . . . MOUNTAIN,
THERE . . .
                ARE . . .
                            BEARS!"

Then he took the iron pot from his father and set it down in the middle of the floor. Now his voice was proud.

"I brought it," he said. "All the way over Hemlock Mountain. And here it is!"